WHAT WILL AUNT TESSA SAY NOW?

Tori turned on the water and adjusted it until it was nice and warm. Then she started spraying Bagel.

As the water penetrated the dog's thick fur, he looked as if he wanted to bolt from the room, but Tori was holding him firmly by the collar. "Good boy. You're going to look so pretty!" she kept saying. He just stood there, quaking, as she worked up the suds. And then . . .

"Look out," yiped Nichelle. But it was too late. Bagel was in motion, shaking off the suds violently.

"Eeek!" screamed Tori as the suds splattered her and everything else in the room — towels, sink, walls, everything.

"Oooo!" groaned Nichelle as a big blob of suds plopped onto her forehead.

"Ahem," said a voice from the doorway. Aunt Tessa was standing just outside the bathroom door.

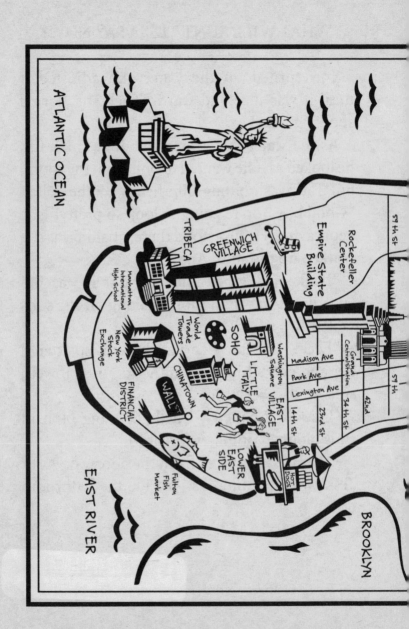

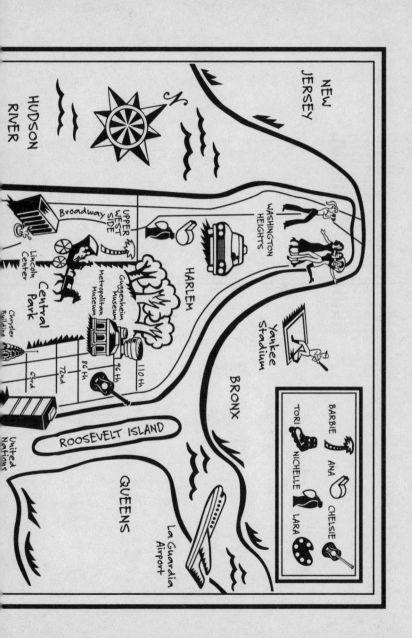

GENERATI*N

GIRL™

#2

Bending

The Rules

By Melanie Stewart

A GOLD KEY PAPERBACK
Golden Books Publishing Company, Inc.
New York

A GOLD KEY Paperback Original

Golden Books Publishing Company, Inc.
888 Seventh Avenue
New York, NY 10106

ISBN: 0-307-23451-7

First Gold Key paperback printing May 1999

10 9 8 7 6 5 4 3 2

Printed in the U.S.A.

GENERATI*N
GIRL ™

Bending
The Rules

Chapter 1

No Skating In The Lobby!

The lobby was cool and dark, like a vast cave, and her skates were fast as lightning on the marble. They made a good sound: *snick, snick, snick.*

As usual, the doorman was having a fit. Louie, this one's name was. A real nervous sort, tall and thin and jumpy. He raised a hand in her direction, just about to give her the usual lecture: No Skating in the Lobby.

"Oh, lighten up, Louie. No worries!" Tori shouted cheerfully in her Australian accent as she sped past him. She flew down over the three small steps and out the door.

And then there was glorious sunlight. Outside at last! Tori Burns threw her arms up to the blue sky and whooped for joy. New York City! She couldn't believe she was here. Her parents had thought that she would be better off halfway around the world from her native Australia. And they were right. Tori loved this huge, hustling, humming city. New York was an extreme place, and she was an extreme girl.

True, it wasn't much fun in Aunt Tessa's big, rambling old Greenwich Village apartment. Tessa herself was no barrel of laughs. Her mouth was so permanently turned down at the corners, there were deep downward-shooting lines there. She worked in the Metropolitan Museum of Art, painstakingly restoring old picture frames. She didn't fool around at work, and she didn't fool around at home. There were so many rules there: Don't make too much noise. Don't stomp around the apartment. Don't sing too loudly while doing the dishes.

And above all, Do not ever, ever, ever go into the three rooms at the end of the long, shadowy hallway. Tori didn't know what was in there, and it was definitely not up for discussion with Aunt Tessa. All Tori knew was that she'd be sent home to Australia immediately if she ever opened one of the doors even a tiny crack. Of course, she was consumed by curiosity. What was the big mystery?

Tori headed west for three blocks on Bank Street. Lost in thought as she sped toward school, she hung a left and skimmed down the bike path that ran next to the Hudson River. Her yellow hair flew out behind her in two long ponytails. Her blue satin jacket was tied around her waist so she could move better.

The guy on the skateboard with the pet monkey on his shoulder waved to her, as he did every morning when they passed each other. He was wearing leather short-shorts, as usual. She waved back, yelled "G'day, mate!" and grinned — this morning the monkey had a red lollipop.

Soon Tori came to a stop at the front steps

of her school. She sat down and quickly changed into her high-tops. It really was an extra-beautiful day. She could see the Statue of Liberty very clearly. It was almost glowing in the strong sunlight. The water in the harbor sparkled.

Streams of kids were pouring into the Manhattan International High School for first period. A few of them waved to Tori as she laced up her sneakers. The Pants Boys, carrying their skateboards, mumbled something and she waved. Tori and her friends gave them that name because of the baggy pants they wore dangerously low on their rear ends. She couldn't remember which one was Evan and which was Andy. Nobody could. But they were both *really* cute, in Tori's opinion.

There were so many kids here! Her old high school at home in Melbourne had about five hundred students; there were at least three thousand at M. I. H. What Tori liked best was that the students came in every size, shape, and color of the rainbow. The bad part was that she sometimes felt like a tiny, insignificant fish in a huge sea. The good part was that it was so huge and diverse, *anybody* could find friends here. She'd only been here for three weeks, and already she had some good mates — Barbie Roberts, Chelsie Peterson, Lara Morelli-Strauss, Nichelle Watson, and Ana Suarez — and she had her eye on a few more prospects. Most of them were sophomores, tenth-graders like herself.

Inside the school it was a madhouse, as usual. Everybody was crowded around the bottom of the escalator or running up the steps two at a time. Since class started in five minutes, she'd have just enough time to check the loose tile on the fifth floor.

"Hi, Tori!"

Tori turned to see Barbie hurrying to catch up with her. "Whew!" panted Barbie. "I thought I was going to be late! There was some kind of tie-up on the subway, and we just sat there in the dark for ten minutes. It was spooky. I don't think I'm ever going to get used to that feeling!"

Barbie wasn't a native New Yorker either. She came from California, and she wasn't yet used to this crazy town. She was trying her best though. Barbie always looked for the best in everybody and everything, which was why Tori liked her. It was true that her style was about as different from Tori's as anyone's could be. Even so, there was just no way you could not love Barbie.

"Do you want to run up to the fifth floor with me?" Tori asked. "I have just enough time to check the tile before I get to English class. Then I'm on my way to French."

"Great, I'll come with you," said Barbie. "I'm on my way up to the fifth floor. I've got to go to history first period." She made a face. "Yuck."

"It's too bad you have Mr. Budge," said Tori. "I know you'd like history more if you had a teacher who was fun."

"It's not him, it's me," said Barbie. "I'm just not very good at it."

"You can be good at it, I know," said Tori. "You just need somebody to help you get excited about history. And Budge isn't the one."

Bending The Rules

Everybody in the school knew about Mr. Budge. He wasn't a mean teacher, he just didn't quite have both oars in the water. He was very smart, but a complete nut for cleanliness. He did not like to be touched. All of his students and even the other teachers knew about his "personal circle." This was an imaginary circle that prohibited anybody from getting closer than two feet from him. If you got too close, he'd admonish, "Personal circle! Personal circle!" In class he talked in a droning voice, writing dates on the board, and he didn't like to answer questions. Not the kind of teacher to get anybody fired up about history.

Tori and Barbie took the escalator to the fifth floor and scooted around the corner to the quiet alcove where the loose floor tile was. Manhattan International High was a brand-new school, and a few things hadn't been finished before school began. Tori and Lara had discovered the loose tile in the second week. It was a perfect place for all of them to leave messages during the school day. As far as they knew, they were the only ones who knew about the loose tile.

Tori wiggled the tile out of its place and looked underneath. There was a little scrap of paper there, and Tori recognized Lara's big, artistic handwriting right away. *Tori*, she'd written with a purple felt-tip pen, *Can you meet me at Eatz for lunch? I have to talk to you about something.*

Eatz was the place where they all hung out when they had a free period. It was only a block from school. Tori thought the food was terrible, but the owners were very nice about letting swarms of boisterous high-school kids fill the booths.

Tori and Lara both had ended up with a ridiculous third-period lunch in their schedules. They often ate together. Third-period lunch meant they had to eat at 10:50 in the morning. So they were usually ravenous by the time they got home.

The crowds in the halls were thinning. Time to run to class.

Bending The Rules

"See you later," Tori said. "Good luck with Budge today. Maybe he'll sparkle for a change."

"Maybe," said Barbie, always hoping for the best. Even though she didn't think there was much of a chance.

Tori thought about Lara's note as she bounded up the stairs to English. What could Lara want to talk to her about?

Chapter 2

In America
They Call It
A Crush

English was interesting, French was boring (all stuff Tori had studied the year before in Australia), and then it was time for lunch. Tori hurried up the street to Eatz, looking for Lara on the way. They only had thirty-eight minutes to eat and get back to school for fourth period. No time to shilly-shally.

Lara was already waiting in one of the tattered orange-vinyl booths when Tori got there, nibbling at a plate of cheese fries and watching the door for Tori. Her waist-length dark hair was gathered into a single braid today. Tori saw she was wearing her multicolored crocheted sweater, over a pink tie-dyed top. Tori loved clothes like that, even though she never wore them.

Tori waved to Bill, the cook, who stood in the window behind the counter and passed food through an opening to the waitresses. Bill was Australian too, and Tori was always happy to see somebody from home.

"G'day, luv!" Bill called to her.

Tori slid into the seat across from Lara, balled up her jacket, and threw it onto the seat beside her. She immediately reached for one of Lara's fries. "What's the word?" she said.

Lara looked a little upset, which was unusual. Normally she looked cool and calm as a mountain pool, never a hair out of place. It had taken Tori a while to get to like her, because they were different in that way; Tori ran hot as fire. But they were also a lot more alike than Tori had first thought. Lara, like Tori, followed

11

her own path. She did not give a hoot what people thought of her shoes, her taste in art, or her ideas. She was her own person. Tori liked that.

It was a good thing Lara was so centered, too, because she'd had a crazy, mixed-up international life that could have made someone else very confused. Her father was German. Her mother was Italian. She'd been raised mostly in Paris, France. And now she was in New York, just sliding into another life without missing a beat.

Tori smiled, thinking about the bumpy start the two of them had gotten off to. They had had a serious misunderstanding on the very first day of school, before they'd even met. Thank goodness Barbie had untangled it before it got out of hand.

Lara pushed a french fry around in a puddle of cheese, but didn't eat it. She looked glumly at Tori. "I think I am a little mixed up," she said in her French-and-whatever-else accent. This was what Tori loved about M. I. H.: Here were an

12

Australian girl and a French girl sitting in a booth, and in the booth behind them were two African boys. Crazy.

"You? Mixed up? Crikey! I didn't think it was possible. What's worrying you?" She ate two of Lara's fries at once.

"Please, have a fry," said Lara with a little smile. "Don't be shy."

"Thanks, I think I will," grinned Tori, taking two more.

"You know my teacher of art history? Mr. Harris?" said Lara. She still had trouble pronouncing the "h," and had to work really hard to get the air out the right way.

"You mean that really really fabulous-looking black-haired one?"

Lara put her chin down on the table and looked mopey. "That is him," she said. "The fabulous-looking one."

"He's a good teacher, right? I remember you told me that. So what's the problem?"

"Oh, yes, he is a very good teacher. He has such a beautiful mind. He understands art better than anybody I know. Everybody wants to be in his class. When he asks you a question, he listens to what you have to say. It is as if nobody else was in the classroom."

"Uh-oh!" said Tori, clapping her hand to her forehead. "I see what the problem is. You can't really have a *crush* on him. Can you?"

"A what?"

"A crush. You know, when you're sweet on somebody. That's what they call it in America. It's very uncool when you have one on a teacher."

"I know. It's ridiculous. I feel as if I am a stupid little girl."

It didn't help that Mr. Harris was Lara's art teacher, either. Art wasn't just a subject for Lara, Tori knew. Although she was maddeningly good at everything she tried, Lara lived for art.

"Come with me to the skateboard park this afternoon," she said to Lara. "They just built some amazing new ramps. The Pants Boys will be there. They're both cute, even if you can't tell which one of them is which."

Lara laughed. "I don't think they are quite my type," she said. "I think I like boys a little more . . . how you say it? — sophisticated. At least they should comb their hair, no? Also, I made a promise with my mom to be home today. You want to come with me?"

Tori always liked going to Lara's house. She lived in a big apartment in Soho. Soho got its name because it was an area south of Houston Street. Lara's apartment was called a loft because there were no walls, just one big open space. Soho was a totally cool neighborhood not too far from Greenwich Village where Tori lived. Full of art galleries, Soho had lots of big, white, spacious stores with polished wood floors and maybe three dresses that sold for a thousand dollars each hanging on a rack. And places with names like "The Center for the Dull." Whatever that was. Every block was full of surprises. It was great!

"I'll tell you what," Tori said. "Let's go to my house first — I mean my Aunt Tessa's house — so I can drop my books off. I'm dragging around my big old biology book today because I had to exchange it for one that doesn't have writing on every page."

"I know. My English book looks like somebody has chewed it up," Lara sympathized. "I have enough trouble with English, without a book that has been chewed." She pushed the fries toward Tori, without having eaten a single one. "Why don't you finish them?" she said. "I'm not hungry."

"That's a bad sign," said Tori. She tried a new approach. "Have you noticed that really good-looking boy in history class? I'm positive he likes you. I wish he would look at me, but it's you he likes. He's obviously attracted to girls who have it all together. Not like me. I have it all apart."

Lara sighed, without even noticing that Tori was trying to make her laugh. "I haven't noticed," she said. She wasn't looking at anybody else besides Mr. Harris, it was clear.

It was time to go back. Lara stood up. "Okay, I'll meet you after school," she said to Tori.

"Oh, just one thing," Tori said as they walked back to school. "You haven't been to my aunt's before, so you don't know the rules. If she's there, we have to be really, really quiet, all right? We can't bother my aunt."

"Oh, okay," said Lara. "Is she sick?"

"No. She just doesn't like to have kids around."

"That's too bad."

"You got that right. See you this arvo."

Lara blinked. "Pardon me?"

"Oh, sorry, it's Australian. See you this afternoon."

Tori watched Lara go up the stairs toward art class. She wondered whether Aunt Tessa would be home, and how it would feel to bring Lara there.

Chapter 3

Lara Breaks The Tessa Barrier

Lara was waiting at the entrance to the tunnel at 3:05. The tunnel, used only by M. I. H. students, connected the school with the bus stop on the other side of West Street.

"Do you want to walk, or take the bus?" Lara asked.

"Let's take the bus," Tori replied. "I'm completely knackered. Gym class took it all out of me. Softball. It's stupid, if you ask me. Give me a skateboard and a killer slope any day. Not this running after the ball."

"Knackered?" Lara asked, confused as usual by Tori's Australianisms. She was confused enough as it was by fast-spoken New York English.

"Oh. Tired," Tori explained. "Bushed. Beat."

"I get the idea," said Lara.

They got onto the bus and hopped off a block from Aunt Tessa's apartment.

"I like this neighborhood," said Lara. "I like your aunt's street."

Tori did, too. It was a mixture of apartment buildings and brownstone houses that made you wonder who lived inside. One of Tori's favorite things to do was to walk along the street in the evenings and look at the lighted-up rooms that didn't have curtains drawn, and see how people lived. A lot of people had walls and walls of books. Aunt Tessa had a lot of books, too. Tori loved that. There were about six books in her parents' house.

There was nothing really *wrong* with Tori's parents. They just wanted a nice girl who would grow up to maybe work in a shop, like Tori's mother, or an office, like her dad. Or she'd be a schoolteacher if she wanted to really go places. People in their family didn't go to college, and they didn't grow up to live far from home. But Tori was different, and Tori's parents simply felt that Tori would be better off at M. I. H.

Louie the doorman was still on duty in the lobby when Tori and Lara came in. He looked very relieved to see Tori walking in on her own two feet.

They waited quite a while for the elevator. When it arrived, out came an extremely fancy-looking woman with a tiny, long-haired dog in her arms. The dog's lower teeth jutted upward, over its upper lip.

"Arf arf arf!" the dog yapped at Tori.

"Arf arf arf arf!" Tori yapped back. The woman gave Tori a sinister look. Tori just smiled pleasantly.

The girls stepped into the elevator. Tori was

about to push 12 when Louie came rushing over. "There's some mail here that I think is for your aunt," he said. "The mailman left it by the mail-boxes, because he wasn't sure. Would you give it to her, please?"

"Sure thing, mate," said Tori.

As they rode up in the elevator, Tori looked at the envelope. She wasn't snooping, it was just idle curiosity, really. She knew so little about her aunt.

The envelope was addressed to "Ms. Tessa Steinmetz." Funny, they'd gotten the first name right, but not the last name. Aunt Tessa's name was Livingstone, same as Tori's mother's maiden name. They'd gotten the apartment number correct, too. The return address in the corner read *Henry Abrams, Abrams Art Galleries,* on Madison Avenue.

Tori opened the apartment door as quietly as she could with her key. This was only the second time she'd brought someone home with her, and the first time no one had been home. Aunt Tessa had never told her she couldn't have anyone over, but Tori didn't feel very comfortable doing it. If she was going to live there for a year, though, she was going to need to bring friends home *sometimes,* wasn't she?

Aunt Tessa was in the kitchen, pouring herself a cup of tea.

"Aunt Tessa," said Tori, "this is my friend Lara. She's only going to be here for a little while, and then we're going to her house, okay?"

"Fine, fine, fine," said Aunt Tessa, waving her hand. She had just a trace of an Australian accent, but she almost sounded American. "How do you do, Lara?"

She didn't really look as if she wanted to know how Lara did.

"Fine, thank you, ma'am," said Lara. "Thank you for having me in your home. It's beautiful."

Wow! Those European kids sure knew their manners. Tori was impressed. Australians were more casual, like Americans.

Aunt Tessa smiled slightly. Her home really was beautiful, not that anybody much saw it. Once in a while, Tori knew, she'd have coffee with a coworker at the museum, but she did not often have visitors. Not many people got to see the beautiful things that filled the apartment.

Tessa herself was also beautiful. Anybody who looked at her could tell she'd been stunning when she was younger. She had high cheekbones, perfect skin, clear blue eyes, and white hair piled up loosely on top of her head. She usually wore exquisite silver and turquoise jewelry from the Southwest — squash-blossom necklaces and long, dangly earrings.

"Would you like to look around?" Aunt Tessa asked Lara. Tori was stunned. Lara must have made a *great* impression. Tori had never seen Tessa be that nice to anybody.

Manners. Very useful. Tori would have to remember that.

"I would love to," said Lara.

They went into the dining room. "The rug is an antique Navaho," Tessa told Lara, pointing to the beautiful geometric-patterned rug underneath the great wooden table.

"It looks like it was made in the late 1800s," said Lara, bending down to inspect it.

Whoa! Tori had no idea Lara knew so much about rugs from the American west. She was amazing.

Aunt Tessa was obviously impressed, too. "That's just about right," she said, smiling. "As far as I know." Tori had never seen a smile that genuine from her aunt. "How do you come to know about Navaho rugs?"

"I am interested in many kinds of art," said Lara. "My mother is a fashion designer — she has a very good eye for whatever is beautiful. I must have inherited my love of art from her."

She crossed the dining room to look at a large painting that was hanging on the opposite wall. It was a painting of a man, very handsome, in a white shirt open at the collar, with the sleeves rolled up. He had a short black beard and very arresting dark, sad eyes.

Lara said nothing, just looked and looked.

Finally she spoke. "This is very good," she

said. "It is special. I do not know the painter. Can you tell me who painted it, please?"

"The painter is forgotten now," said Aunt Tessa. She turned on her heel and walked away.

Tori and Lara exchanged looks, and followed her into the living room.

"Good night! Good night!"

Lara jumped about a foot as the words loudly reverberated through the room.

Tori laughed. "Oh, that's just Waldo," she said. "Aunt Tessa's parrot. She's had him for a million years. I don't know why he keeps saying that."

The girls walked over to Waldo's big cage. He just ruffled his shiny green feathers and gave them a beady-eyed look. "Good night, Ernest," he said suddenly in his rasping voice.

"Does Ernest live here?" asked Lara.

"No. I don't know who he is," said Tori with a shrug. "He just says that sometimes."

Aunt Tessa was busy brushing the dust off a wooden sculpture of a dancing woman in the corner. She was clearly not going to offer any answers to the question of Waldo's utterances.

"Oh, Aunt Tessa, I almost forgot," said Tori, handing her aunt the letter. She'd just remembered she was holding it.

Tessa frowned at the return address. "This isn't for me," she said quickly. "I don't know why it was delivered here. Take it back downstairs with you and give it to the doorman, please."

"Sure," said Tori, a bit mystified.

Since Tori had to drop off her biology book in her room, she took Lara to see it. It was a lovely guest room, large and sunny and filled with rough-hewn, southwestern style furniture. It also had a Navaho rug on the floor, and a handwoven cover for the secondhand computer Tori had bought when she'd arrived. Tori tried hard to keep the room neat, even though it was a struggle for her. At home, she'd always just thrown her clothes on the floor. That meant they were always handy when she needed them. It worked fine for her. But here at her aunt's house, she didn't feel she could do that. She tried to remember to hang everything up. It did not come naturally.

"I think your aunt is very nice," Lara whispered when the door was closed.

"She sure was nice to you," said Tori. "That was amazing."

"Maybe she just needs to get to know you," said Lara. "After all, she has not had anyone else living in her house for a long time."

"I guess that's true. It's probably hard to have a teenager just walk into your life with all her stuff and her music and everything. Especially a teenager who's not yours."

"Is she your mother's sister, or your father's?"

"She's my mother's older sister. I never knew much about her before. She's been living in the States for a long time. I think she had some kind of big falling-out with most of the family, but nobody talks about it much. I could always tell from the way my mother talked about her that she really loves Tessa. But they're just so different. It's hard to imagine they came from the same family." Tori's mother's idea of art was the little ceramic figures of shepherd girls and boys she had in the curio cabinet at home.

"It's nice that you're getting a chance to get to know her," said Lara.

"I guess," said Tori. She stared out the window for a while. "I just don't think she likes me very much."

* * * *

When Tori returned home for the night, she sat down at her desk. In the top drawer was a little pile of postcards she'd bought when she'd arrived in New York. She looked at them all, and then selected the one with the picture of the Empire State Building at night. She knew her parents would like it. It was safer than the one with the photo of the dog wearing boots and a raincoat. She thought for a long time about what to write, and then she sighed.

Dear Mum and Dad,

I am happy and doing well, and I hope you are the same. Aunt Tessa is being kind to me. I am watching my manners. I like my new school very much. New York is a very interesting place. It's not much like Melbourne. How are you both, and how is Bungee? Even though he's only a cat, I do miss him. Please give him a hug for me.

  Love,
  Tori

Chapter 4

Bagel

Tori was not one to brood on the hard parts of her life. She didn't brood at home in Australia, and she certainly wasn't going to do it here. She loved life too much. There was too much to do, too many new things to learn. There was too much fun to have. If she wasn't going to have fun at Aunt Tessa's, she could have fun everywhere else.

School was great. Not that all the teachers were fabulous, but she had enough good ones that she felt as if she could learn something here. Every day she was amazed at how an American school could be so different, and yet so much like school in Australia.

She loved her new friends. She already felt as if she'd known Barbie, Lara, Nichelle, Ana, and Chelsie forever. She knew they would stick by her through thick and thin, and she would do the same for any of them. She had never had a group of friends who were so different from one another, and she loved that. Things never got boring.

The best part of the day was the time she spent in the newspaper office, Room 712. It had no windows and it wasn't very big, but it was bursting with kids, computers, and laughter at almost any time of the school day. Tori sprinted up there when she had a free period, or when there was a substitute teacher who let her go, and, of course, almost every day after school.

Because she loved to hang out in Room 712 and she was so good on computers, she had gradually become the person who was more or less in charge of the school's brand-new website. She was learning how to set it up as she went along. But she was passionately interested in how the web worked. She wanted to make it the coolest website of any school in the world. She worked tirelessly on the graphics, making them brighter and better. She added lots of links to extreme-sports websites, just for her own amusement. And she kept adding new photos taken by the newspaper's staff photographers. Most of the best photos were taken by Barbie. Everybody already knew she was the best photographer in the school, even better than the seniors.

After school, there was always a ton of homework. The teachers at M. I. H. were known for giving lots of it. Most kids, including Tori, usually did their homework with friends. It was more fun that way. She spent lots of time at her friends' houses, especially Barbie's and Lara's. It was easier going there than trying to have people over at Aunt Tessa's.

Luckily, Tori was pretty fast at getting through

her schoolwork, so she still had some time to do the extreme sports she loved so much. She skated. She skateboarded. She played fast, furious handball against the walls in the park with friends from school. And when she needed to think, she'd go over to the rock-climbing wall at Chelsea Piers, the big sports club not far from her house. She'd climb to the top and just hang there and think for a while.

And that's where she was one Saturday afternoon, not long after Lara's visit. Tori was thinking about her aunt, which was something she did a lot. She hung there, facing the rock wall, trying to figure things out. She wished she could understand Tessa better. Tessa wasn't exactly mean to her; she just didn't seem in any way to be open to her. For instance, there was never any possibility of a heart-to-heart talk with her aunt. She knew nothing about Tessa's life. *Why did she have all that southwestern stuff?* Tori wondered. *Had she ever lived there? Or had she always lived in New York? And why did she have so little to do with her family in Australia? And why had she clammed up so fast when Lara had asked about the painting?*

"Excuse me, up there!"

Tori kept thinking, not noticing the voice from below.

"Excuse me!"

Tori looked down. There was the woman who worked there, still holding her ropes at the bottom and looking pretty irritated. "Other people need the equipment, you know!"

"Oh, sorry," said Tori, scrambling down the side of the rock. "I just got a bit lost in thought." She bounced a little when she hit the ground.

"So it appears," said the woman.

Tori clapped the chalky rosin off her hands, apologized again, changed into street shoes, and headed for home.

At Fifteenth Street and Ninth Avenue, she was roused from her thoughts by the screeching of brakes.

"Hey, move it, pooch!" somebody yelled out of a truck window.

Tori looked down the street, and there was a little black mutt with brown feet and a white chest. It couldn't have been more than six months old. It was standing now in the middle of Fifteenth Street, too scared to move. Cars were backed up behind it, honking.

She approached the dog slowly, carefully. "Hey, little guy," she said softly. "Or little girl, whatever. Why don't you come over here and say g'day to me?"

The dog stood paralyzed with fear. Tori squatted down on the sidewalk. She knew if she went over to the dog, it would run away.

"Where's your owner, little one, eh? Don't be afraid. You can come over to me."

The dog eyed her doubtfully.

Feeling in her jacket pocket, Tori found the remnants of a bagel she'd eaten half of at lunchtime.

"Bet you're hungry, aren't you?" she said to the dog. "Well, I have something just for you.

Why don't you come over and get it?"

Now twenty cars were honking behind the dog. Tori stood up. "Be quiet, you boofheads!" she yelled, using one of her favorite insults from home. "Hang on a tick! Can't you see there's animal rescue work going on here?"

She crouched down again. "We're going to have to wrap this thing up here," she said gently. "C'mon over and get this bagel. You know you want it."

Very slowly, the dog began to move toward her. Tori was afraid to move a muscle for fear of scaring it.

Someone yelled, and the dog froze again.

"Come on," Tori coaxed. "You can do it. Good doggie."

The dog kept inching toward her as she held her breath. At last, it was close enough so she could grab it by its collar.

"Sorry, doggie," she apologized as she walked him over to the sidewalk. "We just have to keep you from getting run over."

The dog sat down, shaking, and she scratched

it behind the ears, holding firmly onto its ratty red leather collar. There was no tag hanging from its loop, nothing to identify an owner. Even loaded with dirt as it was, the dog's fur was wonderfully silky. It just needed a good wash, and then a careful brushing. This dog had been out on the street for a while.

Finally the dog stopped shaking so much, looked up, and licked her under her chin. Tori broke into a smile. "That's it!" she said. "We're buddies, right?"

Now. About this little dog, Tori wondered. She'd gotten it out of the traffic, but now what? She couldn't just leave it here. Now she was responsible for it.

A woman with a briefcase walked past. "Would you like a cute dog, Miss?" Tori asked her. The woman didn't even answer, just kept walking.

"G'darn, you'd think I was asking her for money," Tori muttered to herself.

A blue-and-white police car had stopped beside her, waiting for the light to change. The policeman who was driving had the window open, his elbow resting on the window ledge.

"Excuse me," Tori said to him. "Would you like a nice doggie to take home? Or maybe to live at the station house?"

The cop smiled. "I'm sorry, we can't have a dog there. And I have two cats at home. Did you find this dog?"

"Just now. Is there a nice place I could take it to be adopted?"

"There's a place," said the cop with a wry smile, "but it's not a nice place."

Tori hugged the dog protectively. "Okay," she said. "Thanks."

Well, that was out. She couldn't take him to the dog pound. Or was he a her? She bent down to have a look.

"Hmmm. I guess you're a boy." The dog looked up at her, begging pathetically for another piece of bagel. "That's what I'll call you," she said, scratching behind his ears. "Bagel. That's your new name."

He wagged his tail.

Chapter 5

Bathtime
For Bagel

"Okay, Bagel, now we're going to have to get you home," Tori told him. "Lord knows what Aunt Tessa is going to think of you. I just hope she likes dogs."

She stood up, still hanging onto his tattered collar. "Now, what are we going to use for a leash?" she mused. "I can't bend over and hold your collar the whole way home, and if I let you go, I know you're going to run away."

He wagged his tail again.

Tori looked around the street for something,

anything, to tie onto him. Nothing. She looked up and down her own body, searching for anything usable. Nothing. Well, there was one thing; the cord that ran around the bottom of her windbreaker to tie it closed. That was going to have to be it, then. She untied the big knot that kept it from pulling out, and worked it through its channel until it was out.

Bagel didn't seem to know what to do at the end of a leash. He pulled this way and that, sniffing everything he could get his nose into.

"You're going to have to do a little better than that," Tori told him. "Hey, you're pulling my arm out!"

She stopped off at a corner grocery store to pick up a couple of cans of dog food. Liver and bacon. He'd have to like that.

She noticed as she came out of the store that he was lifting his leg against the fire hydrant she'd tied him to. So, at least he seemed to be housebroken. Thank goodness. One problem she didn't have to worry about.

She walked east and turned south on Eighth

Avenue. About half a block ahead of her, she suddenly spotted a familiar figure — at least, it looked familiar from behind. She took a chance that she was right and yelled, "NICHELLE!" About four people turned and looked at her, but Tori was not one to be embarrassed. "YO!" she yelled again, using a New Yorkism she'd quickly grown to love. "NICHELLE! TURN AROUND!"

The tall, beautiful figure turned around, and it was indeed Nichelle, one of her best friends from school. Tori caught up to her in a moment. As soon as she was beside her, she could smell the delicious fragrance that always enveloped Nichelle: Tea Rose.

"What are you doing all the way downtown on a Saturday?" Tori asked her friend. She knew Nichelle lived all the way uptown, in a gorgeous brownstone house in Harlem. She'd already gone there a couple of times to do homework with Nichelle.

"I wanted to go to that great secondhand clothing store on Thirteenth Street," said

Nichelle. "I saw this silk shawl in the window the other day — it was *da bomb*! It had big roses, and six-inch fringe. It was only ten bucks. The moment I saw it I knew I had to have it." Nichelle, with her talents as a model, could make a great-looking outfit out of practically nothing. Tori, on the other hand, was only interested in clothes that she could beat up.

Nichelle finally looked down. She jumped. "Girl, what do you have there?" she said in amazement.

"Most people would call it a dog," grinned Tori. Bagel wagged his tail enthusiastically at Nichelle.

"Yeah, whatever. But what are *you* doing with it?"

"Well, I sort of found him. And now I'm sort of stuck with him. Want him?"

Nichelle shook her head. "My mom's allergic to anything that barks or meows. That pretty much leaves me with anything that croaks."

"I think *my aunt's* going to croak when she sees what I've brought home," said Tori.

"Uh-oh," said Nichelle.

"You want to come with me? My aunt won't be able to murder me if there's a witness."

Nichelle thought about it for a moment. "I guess I could," she said. "I don't have that much homework this weekend. I could come over for a little while."

"Get your best manners out," said Tori. She told Nichelle about how Lara's manners had snowed Aunt Tessa.

"Oh, wait till you see my manners," Nichelle laughed. "My grandma does not fool around when it comes to manners. By the time I was two I could say 'Yes, ma'am' and 'No, ma'am.'"

"Wow!" said Tori. "If I remember to say 'thanks for the grub,' I think I'm doing well."

They stopped by the secondhand clothing shop, but the shawl was gone.

When they walked into Aunt Tessa's building, Tori found Frank, the other doorman, there. He was short and stubby, unlike Louie, but in all other ways they were the same.

Bagel was straining mightily on the leash, all

excited to be in this new and wonderful place. He pulled toward the doorman's legs and sniffed him up and down. The doorman recoiled. "Miss, you're not going to bring that dog in here, are you?" he asked nervously. "It, uh, smells."

"It won't smell for long," she said. "It's a him. His name is Bagel. And he's much nicer than all those fancy-dancy dogs, *I* think."

The doorman just looked doubtful as she and Nichelle sailed past.

Upstairs, Aunt Tessa wasn't home. She was probably out at a poetry reading; she often went to them. Tori half-wished her aunt would invite her along to one, but she didn't feel that she could ask.

The first thing Tori did was put down a big bowl of water in the kitchen for Bagel. "I'll bet you're thirsty," she said.

Bagel greedily lapped up the entire bowl. "I guess you bet right," Nichelle laughed.

Next Tori opened one of the cans of dog

food. The dog scarfed it up as if he'd never seen food in his life. "Poor little guy," Tori said.

When he was done eating, he gave her a little lick on her chin as if to say "thank you." She crouched down and petted him. When she scratched behind his ears, he turned his head so far toward the happy sensation, his head was almost upside-down.

"Well, you sure found a dog who knows how to make people love him," said Nichelle.

Tori knew her friend was right. She was starting to love this dog already. This was very bad.

It was time to get stern. "We're not done with you yet, Mister," said Tori, standing up. "It's into the bathtub with you."

She led him, still on the windbreaker cord, through the living room on the way to the bathroom. Waldo perked up when they entered the room. "Hiya! Hiya!" he said, regarding the dog with great interest.

Nichelle jumped. "Who's *that?*" she said.

"Oh, that's just Waldo, Aunt Tessa's parrot," said Tori. "I hope he likes dogs."

Before they went into the bathroom, Tori changed into a ratty old pair of sweats. She knew she was not going to be dry at the end of this process. "Okay, Bagel," she said as firmly as she could. "It's time to get clean." She patted the inside of the bathtub, and he seemed to know just what she wanted from him. He jumped into the tub and waited for whatever was coming next.

"He's a smart little fellow," Nichelle observed from the farthest corner of the room she could find to stand in.

Aunt Tessa had a shower-massager that came on a sort of long metal hose affair, which was going to make the whole thing a lot easier. Tori turned on the water and adjusted it until it was nice and warm. Then she started spraying Bagel.

As the water penetrated his thick fur, he looked more and more forlorn, and more and more silly. He looked as if he wanted to bolt from the room, but Tori was holding him firmly by the collar. "Good boy!" she kept saying. "You're going to be so pretty!" She lathered him up with the baby shampoo she used for herself; that probably wouldn't be too bad for his skin, she figured. He just stood there, quaking, as she worked up the suds. And then . . .

"Look out!" yipped Nichelle. But it was too late to look out. Bagel was in motion, violently shaking himself off.

"Aack!" shouted Tori as the suds spattered her and everything else in the room as well — towels, sink, walls, everything.

"Oooo! That Bagel is something else!" Nichelle groaned as a big blob of suds plopped onto her forehead.

"Ahem," said a voice from the doorway.

Chapter 6

Bagel Makes A Friend, Sort Of

Uh-oh.

Aunt Tessa was standing just outside the bathroom door, carrying a pile of books from the library. She was silent, just taking in the whole scene.

"Oh! Aunt Tessa!" said Tori, who couldn't think of anything else to say but state the obvious.

"Good afternoon," said Aunt Tessa.

Tori wiped the suds off her face with a wet sleeve. "Aunt Tessa, I can explain all this," she began, wondering if she could.

"Please do," said her aunt. Could Tori be imagining it, or was there just the tiniest hint of a smile at the left corner of Aunt Tessa's mouth?

"Um — first, I'd better introduce Nichelle," said Tori, mostly to herself. "Aunt Tessa, this is my friend Nichelle, from school."

"How do you do, ma'am," said Nichelle.

Way to go, Nichelle!

"And would you like to introduce me to your other friend?" asked Aunt Tessa.

When Bagel saw that Aunt Tessa had her eyes on him, he began to wag his tail, hard, spattering even more lather.

"This is, um, Bagel," said Tori. Suddenly the name sounded a little ridiculous to her. "I found him on the street. I-I couldn't just let him get run over by a car, could I?"

Aunt Tessa sighed. "No, I suppose you couldn't." She put her stack of books carefully down on the small table in the hallway outside the bathroom. Then she came into the room, crossed over to the bathtub, leaned down, and put out her hand for Bagel's paw, which he eagerly offered. She shook his paw solemnly. "How do you do, Bagel," she said. "If you chew my belongings or pee on my rugs, I will murder you, and your young mistress too." Bagel wagged as if his life depended on it, which it probably did.

Tori couldn't believe her ears. "Does that mean I can keep the little bloke?" she said eagerly. "I mean, just until I can find him a home, that is."

"I suppose so," said Aunt Tessa, wiping her hands. "You can't very well put him out on the street again. And the dog pound . . ." She shuddered. "But listen to me very clearly. This dog is your responsibility. You will walk him. You will feed him. You will play with him. And if he chews anything up, I will hold you responsible, and it will probably take until you're as old as I am now to pay for one of these rugs. Understood?"

"Understood," said Tori. She couldn't quite tell if she felt more relieved or scared. "He seems to be a very good dog. Really. He's house-broken and everything."

"That's a very good start," said Aunt Tessa. "He'll stay in your room when you're out of the house. I suggest you roll the rug up, if you don't want to spend your adult years in the poor-house."

"I will," Tori promised. "I'll take such good care of him."

"Good," said Aunt Tessa. She nodded to Nichelle and left the room.

Tori collapsed in a heap on the bathroom floor. "Whoo!" she breathed. "I thought we were toast for sure!"

"But we're still alive, and so is Bagel," said Nichelle. "We'd better rinse and dry him off before he totally soaks the bathroom."

After they towel-dried him, they fluffed him up with Tori's blow-dryer. Now he looked really pretty! He almost seemed to be smiling as he stood there, wagging for all he was worth. His fur was silky and shiny, and his teeth were very white and sharp; he was still a little kid, as dogs went.

There was a brief knock on the door, and Aunt Tessa entered. In her hand was a braided leather leash, beautifully made. "I dug this up for you," she said. "It's from a dog . . . I once had." Her voice seemed to catch ever so slightly when she said it. But before Tori could ask her — *What dog? When?* — her aunt had closed the door and gone.

Tori and Nichelle just shrugged at each other.

"Thank you, Aunt Tessa!" Tori yelled through the door.

Clipping the leash onto Bagel's collar, which was now also a lot cleaner, the girls led him down the hall to Tori's room. He sniffed and sniffed, his nose glued to every inch of the floor.

Down the hall, Nichelle could see the three closed doors. Before Tori could stop her, Nichelle was heading right for them.

"What are these rooms?" she asked curiously.

"*Wait!*" yelled Tori. "Don't go in there!"

"Oh, sorry," said Nichelle. "What's in there?"

"I dunno," whispered Tori. "I'm not allowed to go in there. It's a big mystery."

"Ooooh, cool," said Nichelle. "Mysteries are meant to be solved, you know."

Tori shook her head doubtfully. "I'm not so sure about this one. She'd kill me if I ever went in there."

Listening to herself, Tori was surprised at her own timid attitude toward Aunt Tessa. She wasn't used to worrying about anybody's rules. Maybe it was because she sensed that her aunt was the first person she'd run up against in her whole life who was as strong-willed as she was. If she ever went head-to-head with Aunt Tessa, it would not be the older woman who backed down.

The phone in Tori's room started ringing. Aunt Tessa had had it installed before Tori arrived. Tori guessed it was partly to be nice, and partly so Tori wouldn't be yakking to her friends in Aunt Tessa's living room.

Tori dived for the phone. "Hello?" she gasped.

"Hi," said Lara. "Were you in the middle of something?"

"Well, sort of. Well, no." She explained to Lara about finding Bagel and then finding Nichelle, and the adventure of the bath.

"So maybe you might be too busy to do something with me tomorrow?"

"What did you have in mind? I probably shouldn't leave Bagel alone in my room for too long until he gets used to it. I'll have to leave him all day on Monday."

"I'm thinking about a short trip to the Museum of Modern Art."

"That would be cool. I haven't been there yet. In fact, I haven't been to any New York museums yet except the Metropolitan Museum, and I'll need about ten more years just to see half of that."

"I have a reason for going there," said Lara. "I have a big project to do for my art history class."

"Oh," said Tori. "The dashing and much-too-old Mr. Harris."

Lara let that one pass. "I am supposed to write a paper on a twentieth-century artist. I have to talk about the artist's life and work, and how they affected each other. I really want to do a good job."

"To impress the dashing and much-too-old Mr. Harris."

Ignoring Tori again, Lara continued. "So I want to find a really interesting and unusual artist at the museum. Somebody different, not like Picasso. Everybody's doing Picasso. It's going to be fun. Do you want to come along?"

"Sure," said Tori. "I think I could leave Mr. Bagel for a couple of hours." She turned to Nichelle. "Want to go the Museum of Modern Art tomorrow with me and Lara?" she asked.

"Can't," said Nichelle. "I have to go to some kind of fancy reception with my mom. My dad's on call tomorrow, and my mom wants some company." Nichelle's mother worked as an aide to the Mayor, and she often had to go to city functions. Sometimes it was a visiting foreign dignitary, sometimes it was a dinner to honor a local somebody or other. Usually she dragged Nichelle's father along, but now and then his work as a doctor at Harlem Children's Hospital gave him a welcome excuse to get out of them.

"Oh, too bad," said Tori. "I'll have fun for you."

"Thanks a load," said Nichelle.

Lara and Tori decided to meet in front of the museum at noon. Tori hung up the phone, not knowing that tomorrow would change everything.

Chapter 7

Surprise In
The Lobby

Bagel was a good boy all night. He slept quietly beside Tori's bed, curled up on a winter parka that Tori had spread out on the floor for him. At seven in the morning she jumped up, suddenly worrying that perhaps he wasn't *that* housebroken. She clipped on his leash and took him downstairs.

Frank was at the door this morning. "Morning, Miss," he said, yawning. He did a double-take when he saw Bagel. "He does look a lot better now, doesn't he?"

Tori just grinned.

When she got back upstairs, Aunt Tessa was up. She was in the kitchen, and Tori could smell toast and coffee.

"Good morning," said her aunt.

"Hi!" said Tori.

"Would you like some breakfast?"

"I'd love some!"

Aunt Tessa looked at Bagel with the same tiny hint of amusement Tori had seen yesterday. Tori was almost daring to hope that her aunt was warming up a little.

"Toast?" Aunt Tessa said to the dog, breaking off a corner and handing it to him. "Don't grab," she said.

Bagel, bless his furry little heart, took the little triangle of toast as delicately as could be from Aunt Tessa's fingers.

"Good boy," she said.

"He really is nice, isn't he?" said Tori hopefully.

"He's not bad," said her aunt drily. "Let's see how he does when you leave him alone."

"I'm going to do that for a little while today," said Tori. "Kind of a practice session. I'm going to the Museum of Modern Art with Lara, the one you met last week."

"I remember her."

She didn't say anything about how nice it was that Tori was going to the museum. They ate their toast and jam in silence.

Tori spent the morning working on French and biology homework. She had to do a biology lab, which was picky, painstaking work, drawing a microscope slide of a leaf. Her lab partner, a girl named Francine, was completely useless. Francine always wore black and put on deep purple, bruised-looking lipstick. She had two rings in her nose and a total of nine in her ears. She never, ever smiled; it seemed to be against her creed. And she never, ever did her biology homework, either, which meant that Tori had to do it all. Francine was too busy hanging out with her depressed, dressed-in-black friends and listening to depressing music. Maybe Tori was a rebel, but she was a cheerful rebel. She didn't have much patience for dramatic misery. She wished she had Chelsie, who was also in the class, for a partner. But Chelsie had a boy named Arturo who wore a plastic pocket protector.

At 11:30, she gave Bagel a hug. "You be good," she told him. "I'm going out for a couple of hours. I'll be right back."

Bagel wagged his tail, but he didn't look so happy.

Lara was standing in front of the museum when Tori got there at twelve on the nose. Beside her was Barbie.

"G'day!" said Tori, surprised and pleased to see her. "What're you doing here?"

"Well, just like you, I haven't had a chance to see a lot of museums in New York yet. So when I talked to Lara on the phone last night, I decided to hitch up with you guys."

"That's great!" said Tori. "You can protect me from any and all stuffy museum vibes."

"This museum's not stuffy at all," said Lara as

they went through the revolving doors. "You'll see."

Inside, the large lobby was packed with people and buzzing with activity. Two big escalators went up to the galleries on the second floor, and the outside sculpture garden could be seen through the back windows.

"This place is awesome!" said Barbie. "I can't wait to see the pictures!"

They showed their student IDs at the desk, paid for their half-price tickets, and went in.

Upstairs, they began to wander from room to room. There was so much to see.

"Wow!" they all said at once, walking into a whole room that exploded with the color and light of Claude Monet's *Water Lilies.*

"Hmmm," they all said in the room full of Jackson Pollock's enormous, drippy paintings.

"Do you get this?" Tori asked Lara. "They look as if somebody just dribbled paint all over them."

"This one's called *One*," said Barbie, looking at the plaque beside it.

"That doesn't help much," said Tori.

"But aren't they kind of exciting to look at?" said Lara. "They're so full of movement and life and energy!"

"It still looks like dribble to me," said Tori.

Lara just rolled her eyes.

Next they stood before a huge Picasso painting of a woman whose image seemed to be fragmented into a thousand different pieces, looked at from a thousand different angles. It was called *Seated Woman*. "*This* is cool," said Tori. "This I can get."

They wandered around for a long time, Tori and Barbie trailing behind Lara as she looked for just the right painter.

"You're just obsessing about this because you want Mr. Harris to fall at your feet," said Tori. "Well, it's not going to happen. You wouldn't even want it to happen, not really."

"I know, I know," said Lara. But she kept looking for the perfect painter.

Barbie had drifted to the far end of the room. "Hey, guys, look at this," she whispered loudly.

They crossed the gallery to see what she was looking at. Before her were two paintings hung beside each other, not very big. But they were wonderful.

The paintings were landscapes. They looked like scenes from a desert, with sand and cactuses and animal skulls bleached in the sun. But nothing in the pictures seemed to be holding still. It was as if waves were traveling through them, making them undulate and ripple from one end to the other.

The three of them stood and looked at the two paintings for a long time.

"This one is a ripper!" said Tori about the painting she was closest to.

"Excuse me?" said Lara.

"It's great! It's excellent! Don't you think?"

"I do think," said Lara. "I love these paintings. I can't help feeling as if I've seen other work by this painter, I just can't think what. It's something about the brushstrokes . . ."

"Let's see who did them," said Barbie, peering at the small lettering on the plaque between the paintings. "T. Steinmetz, 1968. Oil on wooden planks."

"Cool," said Tori. "He painted on wood."

"Or she," said Lara. "We don't know who T. Steinmetz is."

Something began nagging at Tori, pulling at her mind the way Bagel pulled on his leash. "Steinmetz, Steinmetz," she said to herself. "Where have I seen that name lately?"

Lara decided that this was the painter she would use for her report, if she could find out more information. "Let's stop at the gift shop downstairs on our way out," she said to her friends. "They have lots of art books down there. Maybe I can find something in one of them."

"Great!" said Tori. She had noticed the gift shop, just off the lobby, as they came in. It looked chock-full of wonderful looking stuff.

They spent another half hour wandering around the museum, stopping for a while at the photography galleries, which they all loved.

"It's so great to look at art," Barbie said as they rode the escalator downstairs. "It just makes you think differently than you do every day, doesn't it? It sort of gets you to see things in a new way."

Her friends agreed completely.

The gift shop was great. Tori chose some stationery that looked as if somebody had crumpled it into a ball and then smoothed it flat, but it was all just a trick of the eye. Barbie bought a super, hi-tech-looking black steel holder for the pens and pencils on her desk. Meanwhile, Lara was in the book area, hunting for any reference she could find to T. Steinmetz.

"Tori! Barbie!" she called. "I found the artist!"

They all gathered around the tremendous Modern Art book, which Lara had opened up on a book display table. There, on the left-hand page, was one of the paintings they'd seen upstairs.

"There isn't very much in the book," said Lara disappointedly. "Here, I'll read it: 'In 1969, T. Steinmetz, an important Arizona painter, abruptly forsook an artistic path that was surely leading to worldwide fame. All but two of Steinmetz's paintings were removed from circulation, bought back by the artist, who then stopped working entirely. A promising talent was lost to the art world, for reasons that are not well understood by art historians.'"

They were all quiet for a moment, staring at the painting in the book. "Wow," said Tori. "What a bummer!"

"Not too good for me, either," said Lara sadly. "There is not enough information, or enough paintings, for me to write my report on. But I really love that art. It is too bad."

All at once, Tori remembered where she'd seen the name Steinmetz. It was on the letter that had been mistakenly delivered to her aunt. What a weird coincidence. Or was it possible that Aunt Tessa knew this artist in some way? She wished she could ask her, but she didn't feel comfortable enough to do it.

Lara closed the huge art book with a thud. It was time to go home.

Bending The Rules

They all parted ways at the Columbus Circle subway stop. Lara had to go one direction downtown on the subway to get home, Tori another, and Barbie was heading uptown. There was still lots of homework to be done before the school week started in the morning.

Tori was also anxious to get home and make sure Bagel had done okay in her absence. This was a sort of dry run, because he'd be alone all day tomorrow. She hoped he hadn't chewed up all her shoes. Or worse, Aunt Tessa's rug. She winced at the thought, and walked a little faster as she entered the lobby to her building.

She was going so fast, in fact, that she almost didn't notice the voices that drifted across the lobby from behind the closed door of the common room. This was the room where the building's board had its meetings. Aunt Tessa's building was a co-op, which meant that the people who lived there came up with the rules about everything that went on in the building. The board was made up of about fifteen people

67

who actually made the rules. They had been elected by all the other tenants in the building. From the way Aunt Tessa sometimes talked about them, Tori got the feeling that a lot of people on the board liked to spend time in the meetings because they needed to get a life.

"But it's so disruptive!" Tori heard someone complain in a harsh voice.

Someone else spoke. "Yes, and it's just not proper, either! We can't have people skating in the lobby. We just can't! If we let her skate in the lobby, what will other people want to do?"

"And if it's not the skating, it's something else. Singing! Doing cartwheels, right down the hallways! And what about that mangy dog she brought home the other day? It probably had all kinds of *insects* living on it!"

"This building does not even allow children, if you'll recall, Ms. Livingstone," said yet another voice in a chilly tone.

Tori was rooted to the spot. She knew she shouldn't stand there listening, but how could she leave? Aunt Tessa was in there, and they were talking about *her!* Were they going to try to kick her out? Would she have to go back to Australia, when she'd hardly even started her life here? Crikey, her aunt must be so mad at her! She felt torn between staying there and eavesdropping on the meeting, and running for her life without looking back.

There was silence in the common room. Tori was in anguish. Then she heard a familiar voice: Her aunt.

"If you'll recall, Mr. Franklin, the rule applies only to children under the age of twelve. Tori is fifteen, well over the allowable age. And I'll tell you something else, all of you. There is not one thing wrong with the child. She has simply got blood running in her veins, unlike the rest of you, it appears. She has a heart that has not yet withered inside her. Can none of you remember what it was like to love every moment of your life, to shout for the joy of it, to do a cartwheel because you can? You should be ashamed of yourselves. You've gotten old and boring!"

There was another long silence, while Tori

stood in the lobby in shock. There was so much to take in. The board wanted to get rid of her! She was fighting mad about that, and upset, too. She'd never dreamed they had such a serious bug about her rollerblading. But her aunt — it was amazing — had stuck up for her, saying astonishing things. Tori had absolutely no idea her aunt had that kind of passion inside her. She'd seemed so severe, so serious, so unfun. But way down deep, there was another Aunt Tessa. And the other Aunt Tessa was a living tornado! Why had she never let Tori see that part of herself, Tori wondered. That part was great. She'd really let them have it. *Go, Aunt Tessa!*

And she liked Tori! She actually liked her. Tori shook her head in wonderment.

Tori snuck over to the elevator and pushed the button, hoping that nobody would come out of the common room and see her there.

As the elevator doors opened, she looked back, just in time to see Louie winking at her.

Chapter 8

T. Steinmetz

Upstairs, Bagel was very, very happy to be let out of Tori's room. He hadn't messed anything up — just twisted Tori's parka into a ball trying to make a nest in it.

She took the puppy into the kitchen right away. "You must be so thirsty!" she said to him as she filled his bowl. She'd have to feed him, too. She only had the one can of dog food left; she'd have to stop off and buy some more tomorrow. She could see where all the money she had saved from her after-school job in Australia was going to go: right into Bagel's little stomach.

Opening the cupboard where she'd stashed the can of dog food, she immediately noticed something new on the bottom shelf. It was a great big green bag of dry dog food. Twenty pounds of it. And not the cheap supermarket stuff, either, but the good stuff from the pet store.

Tori sat down on the floor in front of the cupboard, tears welling in her eyes. She was overwhelmed.

Bagel was not overwhelmed, though. He was just hungry, and he could smell what was in the bag from across the kitchen. He raced to Tori's side, licked her face once, and then began poking at the bag with his nose.

Tori stood up and wiped her eyes with her sleeve. "You're a lucky little bloke," she said to him as she poured out a bowlful of food for him. "Look what your Aunt Tessa bought you.

guess she likes you. I guess maybe she likes both of us."

"She does, just a bit," said Aunt Tessa from the doorway. "But don't get a swelled head about it."

"Aunt Tessa!" cried Tori. She flew to her aunt and threw her arms around her. Her aunt was no hugger, though. She disengaged herself as quickly as possible.

"Bagel seemed very lonely in your room while you were gone," she said, "so I let him putter around the apartment with me for a while. He was rather good company. Waldo took to him, I think."

"Thank you, Aunt Tessa!"

"Don't thank me too much. I don't want you to think you needn't keep looking for a home for him."

"I mean . . ." Tori looked down, anywhere but at her aunt. "Thanks for everything."

There was a moment of awkward silence. "Well," said Aunt Tessa. And that was all.

They were startled by a banging sound that

was being produced by Bagel, who was whacking his tail insistently against the kitchen garbage can nearby. He was looking intently at the countertop where Tori, in her surprise at seeing her aunt, had left the bowl of dog food.

Both of them laughed, and then Tori put the bowl down on the floor, much to Bagel's joy. He tore into the food as if there were no tomorrow.

Tori and her aunt stood and watched him eat, taking pleasure in watching this little dog eating dog food from a bowl, instead of old food from a garbage can outside.

"Bagel is not very popular with the board of this building," said Aunt Tessa.

Tori said nothing. She didn't want her aunt to know she'd been eavesdropping.

"And neither are you," Aunt Tessa added in a dry tone.

Tori searched her aunt's face for clues. Should she apologize? Should she promise to be different? She did feel really bad that her aunt had had to defend her like that in front of those pompous old boofs. But she didn't feel bad about being who she was.

Her dilemma was resolved by a sudden loud buzz beside her ear, which caused her to jump about a foot. It was the doorman calling from downstairs over the intercom, a small white box on the wall near the doorway.

Tori had no idea how to work the thing, since nobody ever came to visit. So she stepped aside and let her aunt do it.

Tessa pushed the bottom button, the red one. "Yes, Louie?" she said into the little speaker.

"Visitor coming up," said Louie's scratchy voice.

"Who is it?" asked Aunt Tessa, stiffening.

"Gee, Ms. Livingstone, he said you were expecting him, so I let him go right up," Louie apologized. "He knew your apartment number and everything."

"I was not expecting anyone," said Aunt Tessa sharply.

"I'm sorry, Ma'am. I won't let it happen again."

"Please don't."

The bell on Aunt Tessa's door rang. Reluctantly, Tessa went to the door, but did not open it.

"Who is it?" she asked warily.

"Tessa, it's Henry Abrams," came the muffled voice from the other side of the door.

Tori stood in the kitchen with Bagel, not quite knowing where she should be. She searched her mind, trying to remember where she had heard that name before.

There was a long pause, and finally Tessa turned the lock, undid the chain, and opened the door.

"Hello, Henry," she said. "It's been a long time."

Aha! That was it. Tori knew where she'd seen his name: On the letter, the one Aunt Tessa wouldn't look at.

"I'm sorry I kind of sneaked up here," said Henry. "But I knew you wouldn't see me if I had the doorman call upstairs first."

"Quite right," said Tessa.

"You know, you can't keep avoiding me forever," said Abrams.

"Why not?"

"Why have you sent back all my letters?"

Now Tori felt really uncomfortable. She felt like she was eavesdropping, standing there in the kitchen. But if she came out, it would be an unwelcome interruption of a difficult moment. She decided to stay. Aunt Tessa knew she was in the kitchen; she'd ask Tori to go to her room if she didn't want her to hear the conversation.

"I have sent back your letters," said Tessa, "because I know what you want from me, and I'm not interested."

"Tessa, it's been almost thirty years. God knows what you've done with all your paintings, but it's time for the world to see them. It's time for T. Steinmetz to come out of hiding, Tessa. You know my gallery will do the best job at mounting a show of your work. Why won't you let it be shown?"

Tori's eyes widened. Aunt Tessa didn't *know* Steinmetz, she *was* Steinmetz!

"Henry, you know better than anyone why I don't work any more, and why my work is not for public viewing. Why can't you just leave me alone?"

"I can't leave you alone. It would be a crime if I didn't keep trying. And I know Ernest wouldn't have wanted this, either. He wouldn't have wanted you to shut yourself away like a hermit. He loved life. He loved art — your art. What is it you do now — fix picture frames or something? It's a joke!"

"I *restore* picture frames, antique ones," said Aunt Tessa. "And it's very important and difficult work."

"I know it's important work," he replied. "But it's not the work you were born to do! Painting is the work you were born to do, and you know it."

"This discussion is over," said Aunt Tessa. "It was nice seeing you, Henry."

"Tessa," he said, "I'm going to leave you my card. I want you to think about this. Don't slam the door on your past. Just think about it."

"All right, Henry. I'll think about it."

"Promise?"

"Promise."

"Then I can leave a little happier. Good-bye, Tessa."

"Good-bye, Henry."

Tori heard the door close, and after a minute she timidly came out of the kitchen, Bagel at her heels.

"I'm — I'm sorry, Aunt Tessa," she said. "I wasn't sure if I should stay in the kitchen, or ..."

Tessa waved her hand. "Oh, it's all right." She looked tired, very tired, and far away. She looked as sad as an empty house after the children and the noise are gone, moved out forever, and only the tattered curtains are left blowing in the breeze.

Tori didn't know what to say. She had so many questions. But was she allowed to ask them? She didn't think so.

* * * *

Before she went to sleep, Tori opened the air-mail envelope that had sat on her desk unopened since yesterday. It was decorated with a pattern of cheerful daisies. Just the sort of thing her mother liked.

Dear Victoria,

Your Dad and I are glad to hear you are doing well. The house is very quiet without you, I must say. All the spring flowers are coming up now, the ones you like so much. We bought a new telly, and it does get a very good picture. I give Bungee a scratch for you every day, and tell him his mistress will be home one day.

Dad and I miss you. Please be careful!

Love,

Mum

Chapter 9

Tori To The Rescue

Aunt Tessa went to her room almost immediately that night and didn't come out. Tori, full of confusion, tried without success to keep her mind on her homework. She walked Bagel at ten, and went to bed soon afterward.

In the morning, Tori didn't see her aunt. She must have gone to work early.

Tori grabbed a piece of toast for breakfast and washed it down with a glass of milk. She gave Bagel a walk down to Hudson Street and back. Then, giving him a good petting, she closed him in her room. "Be strong," she said. "I'll be home before you know it."

Everybody seemed draggy in school that day. It was a drizzly day, and a Monday to boot. Even Mr. Toussaint, her first-period English teacher, wasn't quite as wonderful and electric as usual. They were reading a very long poem by Shakespeare. It wasn't easy to understand, and it didn't seem to make any more sense by the end of the class.

Her friend Ana Suarez, sitting beside her, was trying hard to pay close attention. Ana loved Mr. Toussaint, as did just about all the kids, except maybe a couple of complete boofheads. But Tori could see that even Ana was struggling to keep from daydreaming.

About five minutes before the class was over, Ana passed Tori a note. It had a funny drawing of a stick figure banging away at a computer with a hammer. *Can you meet me in 712 after school?* said the note. *I need major help with the computer! If you don't help me, one of us is going to die, the computer or me!*

Tori flashed a grin at Ana and whispered "no problem, mate." She'd planned to stop by the newspaper office anyhow.

Ana was an amazing athlete. Running, biking, and swimming were her thing, not computers. She didn't have much patience when things went wrong with the computers in the school's newspaper and website office. There was always some practice she was supposed to be at, so Ana needed to run in there, file her sports stories, and run out.

And if she ever did decide to take a hammer to one of the machines, that thing would be plastic dust in no time. Ana had serious muscles. Tori wasn't particuarly interested in the kinds of organized sports that attracted Ana — she herself was more into sports that were extreme or out there — but she definitely respected Ana's athleticism and determination.

After English, the day was pretty much a

blur. French, rainy lunchtime with Lara in the school cafeteria, maths, history, art class, biology, and finally the last bell. Tori raced up to room 712, eager to see what kind of fun was happening there. She couldn't stay long because she had to get home and take care of Bagel.

On the way up to the seventh floor, Tori ran into Poogy, the school custodian. Everybody loved stocky, sandy-haired Poogy. His real name was Boris Pugachev, but nobody ever used that, not even Ms. Simmons, the school principal. Poogy came from Russia. He was working as hard as he could, making money to bring his family over. It was rumored that he had been an architect in his native country, but nobody knew for sure. He'd had to start again from the bottom in his adopted land. But Poogy hadn't let life get him down. He loved America, and he loved M. I. H. He knew a lot of the students' names, even by the third week of school. And he was always there to help when things went wrong, as they often did in the brand-new school building. If it wasn't the escalators, it was the water fountains or the heating system or the toilets.

"Poogy!" Tori cried when she spied him. "I have the best idea for you!"

"What is it?" said Poogy in his heavy accent.

"I know your family isn't in the States yet. So you need somebody to love until your family gets here!"

Poogy started backing away. "Who is it?" he said unhappily.

"It's a dog! A cute little dog! I found him. He's really friendly, and he's housebroken, and—"

"He breaks my house?" said Poogy, horrified.

"Oh, no," she laughed. "It means he doesn't go to the bathroom in the house."

"Oh. Okay."

"Okay, you'll take him?"

"No, just okay, I understand. I cannot take the dog, Tori. Where I live I cannot have dog. I am sorry."

Tori's face fell. "Okay, Poogy. I understand."

"Maybe you put up some posters, yes? Maybe somebody else will want this dog."

"That's a great idea!"

"Maybe you make them on the computer, yes?"

"Yes! I make them on the computer!"

"Okay!"

"Okay!"

Tori gave Poogy a high five and then hustled up to Room 712. She could start making the poster right away, get a really nice one designed. Then she'd ask Barbie or Lara to take a black-and-white picture of Bagel looking his cutest. She'd scan it into the computer and then plop it right into the middle of the poster, nice and big. The poster would look so great, she'd have a million takers, she was sure. She'd just have to choose the very best owner for him, because Bagel deserved the very best.

When she got up to 712, she saw there was a nice new sign on the door — *M. I. H. Generation Beat.* Inside, however, things were in chaos. There were about a dozen kids jammed into the small, windowless room. The kids were all clustered around Chelsie Peterson. Everybody was yelling and screaming. And between the kids and the computers, it was hot in there.

Chelsie was sitting at her computer screen, and Tori was glad there weren't any windows in the room, because Chelsie looked as if she would have jumped out one if she could.

Chelsie had been given the job of Assistant Managing Editor for the paper. That meant she had to edit a lot of the stories, write some of them, and make sure everything was finished and out to the printer on time. In some ways, it was the worst possible job for Chelsie. She was a truly wonderful writer, maybe the best in the school, but she was a sensitive soul. She wasn't very organized and she didn't deal well with pressure.

At the moment, everybody was yelling things at Chelsie:

"Try hitting the escape button!"

"Just give it a good smack on top!"

"Somebody call Mr. Toussaint! Maybe he'll know what to do!"

Tori threw her bookbag onto an empty chair and strolled over to her friend. The crowd parted to let her through. Here was the person who could fix things — maybe. Everybody knew Tori was a whiz with computers.

"Hey, Chelse. What's up?" said Tori.

Chelsie looked up at her, her eyes beginning to brim with tears. Her long, curly auburn hair seemed frizzled with anxiety. "Oh, Tori, I'm so glad you're here!" she said in her lovely British accent. "Everything's in a mess, and it's all my fault!"

"No worries, mate!" said Tori. "It's probably not your fault, and we can probably fix it. Now, tell me what happened."

Ana, who had just come in, made her way over to Chelsie and gave her a hug from behind. "Tori's going to make everything okay," she said in a soft voice. "You'll see."

"I don't know," said Chelsie tearily. "If I lose this story I'm in big trouble. It's the lead story for the paper, and we have to go to press tomorrow morning! Even if I stayed up all night, I don't know if I could do it again."

Ana gulped and hugged her again.

"Okay, Chelsie. Try clicking up there on the left. See if you can get a menu on the screen," said Tori, looking over her shoulder.

Chelsie clicked and clicked. Nothing.

"Hmmm. I see your screen is frozen," Tori remarked.

"That's the problem! No matter what I do, nothing happens."

Tori leaned over and put her ear down to the computer.

"What are you doing, Tori?" Ana asked in surprise.

"I'm listening to see if it's thinking. I want to hear if the hard drive is going. I think it's not. It's fainted. Chelsie, do you have this file on a disk?"

"No!" wailed Chelsie. "I know I'm supposed to, but I always forget!"

Tori stood up and addressed the crowd of

sweaty kids. "Everybody!" she said. "Listen up, and learn from the horror before you. Save everything onto disks! All the time!"

They all hung their heads in shame.

Tori returned to the task at hand. "Chelsie," she said as gently as she could, "have you saved this story at all since you started working on it?"

"I did save it once. I came up at lunchtime to work on it, and I saved it then."

"That's good," said Tori. "Then she's apples."

"I beg your pardon?"

"Oh, sorry. Australian. Everything's going to be okay. As long as the file has a name, we can pull this out. Chelsie, I want you to turn off your computer."

"Turn it off? Then everything will be gone for good!"

"Nope. We're going to make it think there's been a power failure. It knows just what to do if there's a power failure."

"Alright," said Chelsie, reaching shakily for the on/off button. "I just hope you're right."

Squeezing her eyes shut, Chelsie pushed the button. The screen went dark. Nobody breathed.

"Now turn it back on again," Tori directed.

Chelsie pushed the button again. There were lots of little whirs and beeps as the computer woke up. Still, no one dared to take a single breath.

A little box came up on the screen. *Backup file exists,* it said. *Do you want to rename it?*

"There's your file," said Tori. "Just give it a new name, and you're golden."

Chelsie slumped over the keyboard in helpless relief, and everybody breathed again. "I'm going to name it Saint Tori," said Chelsie.

"Maybe you better call it something a bit more sensible," grinned Tori.

Chelsie gave the file a name, and there it was, *bang,* on the screen, as if nothing had ever happened.

"You *are* the *girl!*" Ana said to Tori.

Tori smiled to herself. "If only I could solve all my problems so easily," she said.

Chapter 10

History Lesson

After making sure Chelsie's story was all there, Tori didn't have time to hang around the office any more. She helped Ana quickly, and decided she'd make the poster tomorrow. Right now she had to go home and walk Bagel.

When she walked in the door of the apartment, she sensed immediately that something wasn't right. What was it?

The lights were on in the living room, that was it. At this time of day, the lights shouldn't have been on. Her aunt didn't usually get home from work until about six, and it was only 4:30. Tori searched her memory: Had she left the living room lamp on this morning? No, she hadn't even turned it on.

"Hiya! Hiya!" That was Waldo, putting his two cents in. Tori didn't think he talked when nobody was home. She decided she'd better go and take a look.

There in the big armchair was Aunt Tessa. She had a glass of red wine in her hand, but she hadn't drunk any of it. She was just staring into space. Bagel lay at her feet. He beat the floor with his tail when he saw Tori, but Tessa did not move.

"Aunt Tessa! Are you okay?" Tori said, alarmed.

Tessa jumped. She'd been so far away, she hadn't even heard Tori. "Oh, I'm all right," she replied. "I guess. I just had a rather awful headache, so I came home from work early."

Tori had already seen Tessa go to work with the flu, so she knew that it took something really bad to make her stay home. She was not the self-indulgent type.

"Can I get you something?" Tori asked her. "Some tea, maybe? Or an aspirin?"

"No, thank you, Tori. I think I just need to . . ." She trailed off without finishing the sentence.

Tori sat down on the sofa. She knew she should probably make herself scarce, but she was too worried about her aunt. Tessa looked exhausted and haggard.

"Aunt Tessa," she said, "can I ask if this has something to do with that man who came last night? That Henry Abrams?"

Her aunt sighed. "I suppose it does, dear," she replied. "I suppose it does."

"Who is he, anyhow?"

"He's a man I knew a long time ago."

"I kind of figured that. But who is he?"

"He used to be an artist, years ago. Not a terribly good one. Now he owns a big art gallery on Madison Avenue."

"And," said Tori, jumping into the deep water now, "he wants to show your work."

"Yes. He does."

"Aunt Tessa, I didn't even know you were an artist! Nobody in the family talks about it back home. Why don't they?"

"I don't think they were very happy with my lifestyle. They didn't understand it very well. They couldn't imagine why I didn't just stay home and get a job in a shop. I think they looked at me as a sort of traitor for striking out on my own."

"I know that one," said Tori with a rueful smile.

Aunt Tessa smiled, too. "I think perhaps that's why they sent you to me," she said. "They don't want to punish you; they just don't know what to do with you. Your parents want you to be happy, you know."

Tori, to her great irritation, felt her throat choking up a little. "Do they?" she said. "I have no idea what they want. And they don't know what I want, either."

"They were young once, too. Did you know that your mother was once suspended from school for dancing the *can-can* in the hall-ways?"

Tori burst out laughing. "She never told me that!" she hooted. "Never!"

Aunt Tessa smiled. "I guess she and your dad just felt they were supposed to be serious after they became parents. They wanted to be the best parents they could, I suppose."

There was a silence. Then Tori spoke. "And what about you, Aunt Tessa? You were a painter. Why did you stop?"

"It's a very long story," said Tessa.

In his cage, Waldo shifted from foot to foot on his perch. Tori watched him, thinking.

"It's all about Ernest, isn't it, Aunt Tessa?" she said at last. "That's what Henry Abrams said: 'Ernest wouldn't have wanted it this way.' Who was he? Is that him in the picture in the dining room?"

Waldo got all excited, hearing a name that he hadn't heard spoken for a very long time. "Good night, Ernest! Good night, Ernest!" he cackled happily.

Bending The Rules

Aunt Tessa sat for a while without speaking, her chin in her hand, her index finger against her lips. Then she stood up and smoothed her gray wool skirt. "I suppose it's not really such a long story after all," she said to Tori. "You might as well know it. Come with me."

With Bagel right at her heels, she led Tori into the dining room, where they stood before the painting of the handsome man. "This is Ernest Steinmetz," she said. "He was a sculptor, a very good sculptor. His work is in museums all over the world. He was my husband."

Tori's eyes widened. "Nobody ever told me you'd been married, either!" she said.

"Well," said her aunt, "as I said, I don't think they had much taste for the way I lived my life. Ernest and I lived in the desert in an artists' colony, a group of houses and studios where everyone lived and worked. Art was all we did, all we talked about, all we cared about. Henry Abrams lived in the colony for a time, but he wasn't built for that kind of life. It was too intense for him. He needed the city and its distractions.

"One day, Ernest was driving to Santa Fe to buy some art supplies. I stayed behind, because I was working on a painting that I was excited about. This painting." She swept her arm toward the wall.

"That night I got a call from the police," she continued. "Ernest had been in an accident. Something involving an oil truck, I never found out exactly what. He wasn't killed, but he was badly injured." Aunt Tessa was forcing herself to keep talking now, although the pain of the memory was almost unbearable. Tori could hardly stand it, either. She knew that if Tessa allowed herself to cry, she would bawl too. But Tessa's eyes were dry, through an act of iron will.

"When they'd done what they could for him, I took him home from the hospital and took care of him. He lived for two more years, but he could never work again. And neither could I.

I finished the portrait of Ernest, and that was the end.

"We had a dog, a big black mutt named Fletcher. Fletcher was about the only thing that could make Ernest smile. About six months after Ernest died, Fletcher died of old age.

"That was it. I made a big fire out in the desert and burned all my paintbrushes. I gave my paints away. And I bought back all the paintings I'd sold to museums and collectors. I erased Tessa Steinmetz the artist from the universe.

"Then I packed up my things, came here, and got the job in the museum. And that, my dear, is the end of the story."

Tori was stunned. She had never heard such a sad story in her life. It was the loneliest story she could imagine. She felt so terrible for her aunt. But she knew by instinct that the worst thing she could do would be to hug Tessa, or to let herself cry. It was hard enough for Tessa to keep herself together without Tori blubbering all over her.

Tori stared up at the painting of Ernest Steinmetz. What a handsome man. What energy he had. What life! What was it Henry Abrams had said? Ernest loved art — Tessa's art. She could see all that Ernest was, just by looking at the painting.

"Aunt Tessa," she said when she could speak again, "where are your paintings?"

"I think you know," said her aunt.

She was right. Tori knew. She just didn't know she knew. She jumped up and flew through the dining room, the living room, and down the hall to where the three forbidden doors stood closed. Bagel followed, barking, and Aunt Tessa came last.

"Which room?" said Tori.

"All of them. Open any door you want," said Aunt Tessa.

Tori turned the knob on the first door, her heart pounding.

At first she couldn't see anything. A musty smell hit her in the face, so strong it was almost solid. It was dark in the room. She felt for a light switch, found one, and flipped it. But the bulb must have been burned out, because nothing happened.

Aunt Tessa slipped into the room behind her. She made her way through the room, feeling each canvas until she reached the window, which had a heavy shade on it. Tori heard the shade fly up, and the room was flooded with slanting afternoon light.

The air was so thick with dust, it took Tori a few moments to adjust. Then she began to make out the paintings: stacks and stacks of them, leaning against every wall. Landscapes. Still-life pictures of fruits, vegetables, flowers. Portraits.

"Are all of the rooms like this?" she asked her aunt.

"Pretty much."

Tori knelt down in front of one painting. It was very much like the ones she'd seen in the Museum of Modern Art, but larger. It had the same feeling of waves moving through the landscape.

Dazed by the dusty magnificence around her, Tori realized that nobody had seen these paintings for thirty years. Not one soul. Aunt Tessa had slammed the book shut on her life as an artist.

Wordlessly, Tori looked through the paintings. There must have been a good fifty in the room, each more wonderful than the last. She particularly liked the portraits. They were of men and women and a couple of children, some of them Mexican people, many of Ernest. They showed such a deep understanding and love of her subjects, it was hard to believe they'd been painted by this severe and distant woman.

"Crikey, Aunt Tessa," said Tori. "It just seems like such a terrible shame that nobody has seen these paintings in all these years but me."

"When I lost Ernest, it was as though a light went out in my life. Can't paint without any light, you know. So it's over."

"But, Aunt Tessa, it doesn't have to be over!

You're going to be living a long time! You're such a great painter! Henry Abrams was right. You weren't meant to spend your time in a little room at the museum, working on picture frames. You're supposed to paint!"

Aunt Tessa was silent, and her silence made Tori feel frustrated. She was starting to get mad.

"You know what I think, Aunt Tessa?" she said, jumping to her feet. "I think you're just like me! All or nothing, that's our motto. My way or no way at all. If I don't like the rules, too bad! Nuts to everybody! And if you don't like the rules, Aunt Tessa, you say nuts to everybody, too.

"But you know what I'm finding out? Sometimes the rules are stupid, like no skating in the lobby. And sometimes the rules are horrible, like people we love have to die. It's not fair, but there it is, and we can't always have things our own way. If I skate in the lobby, it just hurts you. And if you stop painting — well, that

103

hurts you, too, and the whole world! So I'll tell you what: I won't skate in the lobby. And you'll be T. Steinmetz again. Deal?"

Tessa remained silent. Tori wasn't angry any more, she was just worried that she'd completely blown it with her aunt. Who was she to give a woman four times her age a lecture like that? What had she ever gone through in life that was a millionth as hard as what Tessa had experienced?

Aunt Tessa smiled. "You're a smart girl, my niece," she said. "Now go and get me Henry Abrams's card."

Chapter 11

Everybody Wins

The T. Steinmetz show opened at the Henry Abrams Art Gallery just after New Year's. Madison Avenue, home to some of the classiest stores and galleries on earth, was still lit up from Christmas, and it sparkled at night like miles of diamonds.

Tori was allowed to invite anyone she wanted for the opening-night party. All her best friends were there: Barbie, Nichelle, Ana, Chelsie, and of course, Lara. (She'd thought about inviting the Pants Boys, but she just didn't think they'd be able to get it together, clothes-wise.) The girls stood around with martini glasses full of ginger ale, trying not to gawk at the glittering crowd of famous people who had come to see the most talked-about show of the year.

"Check it out! There's Madonna!" whispered Ana, nudging Tori wildly in the ribs. "I think so, anyway. What color is her hair this week?"

"Wait, I'm busy looking at those two women over there," Tori whispered back. "I think they're supermodels or something. Did you ever see anybody so tall in your life?" She herself was feeling much taller than she ought to be, in uncomfortable high heels and a little black dress borrowed from Barbie.

Nearby, a guy from the local TV news station was interviewing Aunt Tessa. The camerawoman held a microphone out on a long stick like a fishing pole. The mike was swaddled in some kind of fuzzy stuff to muffle the noise. Aunt Tessa looked dazzling in a long midnight-blue silk dress and dangling diamond earrings that Tiffany's had lent her for the night, just so lots of people would see them on the news.

"Ms. Steinmetz," the news guy was saying, "what made you decide to let the public see your paintings now, after all these years?"

Aunt Tessa smiled radiantly. "Sometimes," she said, "people change their minds. And sometimes people need other people to help them change." She was looking right at Tori when she said it. Was that the tiniest wink, or had Tori imagined it?

Henry Abrams came up to Tori, a real martini in his hand. He clinked glasses with Tori. "Well, I never thought I would see this day," he said. "And if it hadn't been for a pain-in-the-neck kid from Australia, I never would have."

"Look at Aunt Tessa," Tori said to him. "Doesn't she look happy?"

"She hasn't looked this happy in thirty years. I don't know what you've done to her, but it's been good medicine."

"I just annoyed her to death," said Tori. They both laughed.

When the television interview was over, Aunt Tessa came over to see how Tori and her friends were doing. "Did you get enough to eat?" she asked the group. "The stuffed mushrooms are very good. But I'd stay away from those dreadful little hot dog things," she added darkly.

"I think they're bonzer!" said Tori, just stuffing the last bit of one of them into her mouth.

Aunt Tessa turned to Lara and gave her a hug. "How did your paper go, dear?" she asked. She and Lara had gotten to be great friends, it was obvious.

"It was *magnifique!*" said Lara. "I'll show it to you when Mr. Harris gives it back to me. I cannot thank you enough for the interview." Not only had Lara gotten an exclusive interview with T. Steinmetz about her life and work, she had gotten her own private viewing of the paintings in the apartment before anybody else but Tori had gotten to see them. If that didn't wow Mr. Harris, nothing would.

"You know, I was thinking, Lara," said Chelsie. "Why don't we put your paper on the

Generation Beat website? It'll make M. I. H. famous. It'll make *you* famous!"

"That," said Tori, "is a bonzer idea. I can do the graphics to make it look really good."

"Mrs. Steinmetz," said Nichelle, "I just have to tell you how much I love your work. I'm so happy I got to see this show."

"Thank you, dear. You know," Aunt Tessa continued, "I've been thinking about doing a little portrait painting. I don't even know what kind of painter I am now. But I'm going to be needing a model. I've had my eye on you. You have beautiful bones in your face, my dear. And you do some modeling work, don't you?"

"Oh, yes!" said Nichelle, scarcely able to contain her excitement. "I do. And I know how to hold still and take direction and everything!"

"Let's talk about it when this excitement dies down," said Tessa. "Perhaps we can work out a little after-school job for you." Nichelle looked as if she was going to faint on the spot.

"Pssst! Look!" Chelsie hissed into Tori's ear. She pointed over to the door, where Mr. Harris was entering with a beautiful redhead on his arm.

When he saw the girls, he waved and steered the woman over to them. Tori introduced him to her aunt, and he told Tessa how happy he was to meet her. "And it was so nice of you to let Lara interview you," he said. "She wrote a wonderful paper." He turned to Lara. "You're getting an A plus, of course," he told her.

"I really enjoyed reading it, too," said the redhead. "It was very good."

"Oh, I'm sorry! I forgot to introduce you," said Mr. Harris. "This is my wife, Rosalynn."

Mr. Harris's wife smiled a lovely smile. Lara smiled a somewhat less enthusiastic smile.

Mr. Harris and his wife returned to conversation with Aunt Tessa, and Tori bent to whisper into Lara's ear. "Well, easy come, easy go," she said softly.

"Easy come, easy go," Lara repeated. "At least I'm getting an A plus." She even managed a little smile.

The gallery stayed packed with party-goers for hours. The girls stayed, soaking up the art and the glamour and the little hot dog things. "This is why I love New York!" said Barbie, waving a stuffed mushroom around at the scene. "You just can't get this anywhere else!"

Finally, at about one in the morning, the crowd began to thin out. By this time, Tori and her friends were sprawling on the carpeted circular stairway that went up to the closed second floor. They had all taken off their uncomfortable heels.

"Boy, I'm beat," said Ana. "It's a good thing I don't have a track meet this weekend."

"And it's a good thing we don't have school tomorrow," added Chelsie.

Aunt Tessa walked out into the lobby with her cape over her arm. "I thought I'd find you here," she said. "I'll treat you all to cab rides home. You all look about done in. And besides," she added, "I've really got to be going home myself. After all, our new dog Bagel has been alone for too long. Don't you think so, Tori?"

Tori just smiled.

* * * *

Tori needed to do just one last thing before she went to sleep that night. She picked out a postcard of the Statue of Liberty from her desk drawer. Then she uncapped her pen and smiled.

Dear Mum and Dad,
*   Things here in New York are getting better all the time. I'm learning a lot, and Aunt Tessa and I are getting along like mad. I am really looking forward to my trip home for the summer, even though it will be winter down there. I have so many things to tell you.*

*   I love you,*
*   Tori*

TURN THE PAGE TO CATCH
THE LATEST BUZZ FROM
THE *GENERATION BEAT* NEWSPAPER.

geNeRATI✳N BeAT

NUMBER OF ABANDONED ANIMALS GROWING

New York is full of dogs and cats that have been abandoned by their human companions. These animals are sometimes very thin, and often sickly.

Tori Burns, a sophomore at Manhattan International High School, recently found a stray dog on West Fifteenth Street.

"Bagel is a great dog," said Tori, "but I think it's terrible to leave a poor, defenseless creature all alone on the street like that. If I hadn't taken Bagel in, who knows what might have happened to him?"

A veterinarian at a neighborhood clinic said that this problem gets worse when people give animals as holiday gifts. At first people love the animals, then they realize they can't care for them.

So, if you are thinking of asking for a dog or cat as a gift this holiday season, be sure you can give it the love and care it deserves.

Gathering Information

As you write a news article, it is important to remember that your goal is to inform your readers. When they have finished reading your article, they must know something new. Before you can write like a journalist, you must first learn to be a detective.

Your job is to think of an interesting idea for an article, research it, and organize your information. Once you have done that, you will find that the writing part is easy!

To write a news article:

• **Think of an idea.** You might hear someone talking about a problem, or read something in a magazine, or see something on television. If you think other people would be interested in this idea, then you can move on to the next step.

• **Research your idea.** The author of the article on stray dogs spoke to Tori Burns and to a veterinarian about the problem. *What every journalist needs to know:* As a reporter use your eyes and ears! Everything  you see and hear can be used to help you write your stories. Don't be afraid to ask questions. Don't be afraid to research information at the library and on the internet. Always take careful notes while doing your research.

• **Reread your notes.** Think carefully about the general idea you are trying to get across. The author of the *Generation Beat* article realized that stray animals are a problem in New York City, and that the problem tends to become worse over the holidays. She used this topic as the main idea of her article.

• **Write the article.** Be sure to answer the "who, what, when, where, why, and how" questions.

• **Ask a friend to read the article.** Did they learn something about the topic?

Have fun! And always remember what Mr. Toussaint says:
WRITING=HONESTY=TRUTH

Look for Book #3 in the exciting
GENERATI✳N GIRL SERIES

Ana is training for the ultimate sports challenge. She's swimming, biking, and running like there's no tomorrow. But she has to face the true test of sportsmanship when Clarissa, her snobby teammate, pushes her to the limit.